THE NORTH SHORE

Donald E. White

ARTHUR H. STOCKWELL LTD
Torrs Park, Ilfracombe, Devon, EX34 8BA
Established 1898
www.ahstockwell.co.uk

© Donald E. White, 2021
First published in Great Britain, 2021

The moral rights of the author have been asserted.

All rights reserved.
No part of this publication may be reproduced
or transmitted in any form or by any means,
electronic or mechanical, including photocopy,
recording, or any information storage and
retrieval system, without permission
in writing from the copyright holder.

British Library Cataloguing-in-Publication Data.
A catalogue record for this book is available
from the British Library.

This is a work of fiction. Names, characters, places and incidents are the product of the author's imagination and any resemblance to actual persons, living or dead, events or locales, is purely coincidental.

ISBN 978-0-7223-5081-2
Printed in Great Britain by
Arthur H. Stockwell Ltd
Torrs Park   Ilfracombe
Devon EX34 8BA

INTRODUCTION

More than 250 years has passed since the last Roman legions left the north of England.

Despite their evacuation, their influence on the settled life of Britain has not entirely disappeared, because legionnaires of several nationalities had taken local girls to wife and raised families. Communities had been reinforced by those legionnaires who had chosen to stay in England when their period of statutory service expired.

By this time these influences were on the wane, but many Roman ideas about discipline and military service still influenced English leaders. In England life at this time was concentrated within small family and village communities, often widely scattered and therefore vulnerable to attack from marauding bands. In the north, most were quite vulnerable to Scots raiders, now called reivers, and, of course, German and Norse raiders from Scandinavia and Northern Germany.

My tale is set at this time in our island life and concerns a small coastal community whose leaders seek alliances to enhance the safety of their people.

CHAPTER 1

The late summer had been kind, warm and golden, but it had been a difficult year for weather and the crops planted in the village plots were poor. The gathering of wild fruits, like sloes, damsons and blackberries, would be necessary and storage of roots and tubers was essential.

The people of this small community were not alone in their troubles. Scots reiver bands were raiding in increasing numbers, so winter preparations were regularly interrupted in order to fend off these marauders.

Rolf's village had been hit several times, and one day when he returned from a successful hunt it was clear they had called again. Cabins, huts and sheds were in flames and the main storage barn was a wreck. This raid was clearly much more destructive than earlier raids. The Scots were a scourge on the people of these shores, but they were seldom destructive for no reason, since they might need to claim their tributes again. This raid must have been carried out by Norsemen, who had no such scruples.

Rolf and his small band all had the same thought: 'Where are our families?'

Frantically he and his team scattered in search of their own kin. The search did not take long. Some alarm must have been given, for many had tried to escape into the surrounding forest, but their bodies lay where they had fallen before reaching safety. Old men, young boys and women lay all around.

Young girls had been taken for service as slaves and probably to trade along the European slave routes to the East.

Rolf stumbled blindly in his searching and soon found his

young wife, currently carrying their first child, amongst the dead women. Many were naked – they had been raped before dispatch. He and his men were howling in grief and cursing the gods who had permitted such atrocities.

Rolf's mind filled with absolute desolation and a manic desire for revenge. Waving his axe and armed also with his bow, he charged off into the forest. Praying for revenge, and intent on finding someone to kill, he moved swiftly like a hunting dog on the scent. The trail of the despoilers was easy to follow and led him over the rising headland and down into the bay beyond.

The dreaded dragon boats lay in the waters of the bay, but were already on their way northwards across the sea. He cried a challenge, screaming in his rage, but the Viking men either did not hear him or had no interest in returning to shore to kill him.

Rolf finally sank to his knees and succumbed to overwhelming sorrow.

CHAPTER 2

Rolf did not want to recover his wits, but nature will not permit a healthy man to stay in the pit of despair for long. He finally began to recover to awareness when the incoming tide washed over his legs. He could not take revenge, and he could no longer raise a curse, so he began to think. He must get back to the village. He must see what needed to be done.

Slowly, painfully, he raised himself up and staggered back along the trail of devastation. By the time he got back, several villagers had reappeared from wherever they had found refuge, including several boys and girls. All were traumatised by what they had witnessed, but the matriarch had organised food and set campfires for warmth burning brightly. With this light, and flames from some of the huts still burning, he could see perhaps thirty folk had survived. They all clamoured for his attention.

Old Sarah, the matriarch, called to them: "Return to your own campfires. Eat, drink and sleep if you can. Tomorrow we will consider what is to be done."

She drew Rolf to her fire, fed him and gave him a potion to make him sleep. He made no demur, glad to be cosseted.

When he awoke the following day, Sarah told him, "You are now the senior male left alive." The former headman, Lund, and his two henchmen had all died. Dana, the oath wife of Lund, had been found. Raped and left for dead, she still lived, but was badly hurt, both physically and mentally. She would live or die according to the will of the gods.

Sarah had ordered that the remaining women should take Dana to the shore, wash her and cleanse her as much as possible. This had been done, and Dana was now being carried to the Woman of the Woods, who might be able to help her. Rolf thanked Sarah for her common sense.

By mid morning all those still alive would gather to consider what was to become of their community, but first they must attend to the dead.

A pall of sadness lay over the village as the smoke and ash from the funeral pyre dissipated. Some took scraps of bone and the ash to retain in pots in family shrines. The hardest to console were those who had lost children. Many grieving mothers were now ageing and no longer fertile. They couldn't give birth to substitutes, even if they were so inclined.

Rolf invited the Woman of the Woods, Loren, to hold a wake, to pray to the gods of the forest and sea and lead them in restoring the impaired village guardians; then he announced three days of general mourning. He reasoned that the people needed time to recover before further rational discussion could take place.

CHAPTER 3

Once all were gathered near the remains of the Hall House, Rolf revealed his thoughts and listed the points needed to be considered if this community was to survive:

1. The exact body count: who had been left alive and able to function?

2. Were there enough families to sustain a community life in the foreseeable future or should they disperse?

3. Food. Winter would arrive quite soon. What reserves had been hidden or hoarded and were still accessible?

All family leaders, male and female, were asked to think, talk with their families and report back to him by the next day. Most reported that their preference was to stay together, so Rolf planned accordingly.

Later, the women of the village were assigned the task of trapping pools of seawater under the cliffs nearby, and drying them to provide salt for curing meat. When enough was available, all pigs except for the healthiest would be slaughtered and salted down. Roots, greens and nuts would have to be gathered and stored too, so a cool underground storage place would have to be identified.

While all this work was going on Rolf and his team roamed and hunted widely.

One day, returning from the salt pans, the young son of Jani spotted a cave-like opening behind the headland. They all set off to explore it, approaching the opening along paths made by foxes.

Using brushwood and straw, they fashioned flambeau-style torches and set out to explore the cave. It was a great find. The opening was quite small, but it opened out into a linked cave system. The first cave was a barnlike vault; the second and third caves were full of debris, but could be cleared and used for storage and sleeping quarters. From the third cave a passage dived down for nigh fifteen feet to a channel that had once carried water to a shallow basin. This was now dry. Everyone commented that the air they breathed was still sweet, so clearly outside air was entering the cave system.

The elders called a gathering, and after a full discussion they agreed that the cave system should be cleared and used as temporary quarters for the seven families over winter. A new safe, defensible village would be built in the spring. All agreed and work was started immediately.

The days of this clan were now very busy. Males worked on clearing rubble from the cave system, then cooking areas were allocated and bench-like beds were arranged in the sleeping quarters. The storage area was made larger, then individual covers were shaped from the limestone to top pots and barrels, as defence against rodents. These would be sealed with beeswax until needed. Storage shelves were created for vegetables and fruits already preserved.

Finally, attention was turned to the public area, where a huge fireplace was created. Smoke would be vented through fissures in the rock, filtered through a complex arrangement of willow branches and dried seaweed bands, then directed skywards and into a wooded ravine. Winds would disperse the smoke nicely from there.

The only drawback remaining to be overcome was the absence of water. Rolf went to see the Woman of the Woods, who told him she would contact a water diviner. With winter fast approaching, contact was made and a price agreed, then the diviner set to work.

The obvious starting point was the old dried-up basin and its former water channel, but no source of water was located in the cave at all. Next the diviner moved to the hillside and mound outside the cave complex. Here there was a series of connected springs, obviously fed in some way from the high hills further inland. Rolf and the diviner decided to investigate why water from these springs had ceased to flow along the old beds. They discovered plenty of water in the ravine behind the hill and worked their way through the wooded slopes until they came to where a landslip had occurred.

Rolf called his able-bodied men, and gradually and painstakingly the rubble and rocks were removed and stacked. They were later used to construct a sort of backdoor viewing post. This had wide-ranging views inland, and far in the distance they could even see along part of the old Roman road.

All this careful work finally brought a reward. As the last fallen pieces were removed, spring water was again seen filling a natural pool. Minutes later, once this pool filled, fresh and potable water once again flowed into the original channel, as it had done in ages past, and on into the cave basin. When full, the basin overflowed into another channel and the water naturally drained away.

Communal joy reigned as their new winter home was now useable, and most of the villagers decided to move from their temporary quarters immediately.

Rolf used his men for one last task. The viewing post was furnished with a new high wall and a firepit, which could be used to aid defence. The springs were individually covered and trees and bushes planted over the culverts to hide them from view.

The remaining families now joined the rest of the clan inside their winter home, and after some initial quarrels (for example, over who slept where), they all decided to feast in celebration. Rolf was confirmed as tribal leader and given pride of place as a reward for his efforts.

The celebratory feast would be consumed under an old oak tree which stood alone in the forest surrounding their new home. An ox and lambs were killed to feed the families. The Woman of the Woods was invited to see that all the rituals due to the Green Man were carried out properly.

The feast period ended after two days and nights, and it was clear that several families would acquire new sons or daughters.

'Good,' thought Rolf.

The Woman of the Woods, Loren, had brought news of Dana too. She was very weak, but appeared to be making a recovery despite her age and condition. Loren was wise in the uses of herbs and other plants and had made potions and salves to heal Dana's wounds. Rest and time to recuperate would do the rest, as the gods willed.

CHAPTER 4

Winter came upon them suddenly. Gales from the east brought unseasonal cold and a lot of snow, so hides were hung to cover the eastern entry and fires were lit in both hearths. Life eased and it was time for some leisure through the long nights. The old tales were told again by men. They recalled their youth and talked of friends who had lost their lives during some great quest or in battle. The women exchanged ideas, told tales of love lost or hearts stolen, and sang songs handed down by their parents from the ancients. Many songs had been passed down for generations, and they rang with fables or yearning for homes across the seas. It was a time of consolidation, of coming together and setting aside the cares and worries of everyday life. Clan histories are so important. The children listened and were transported too.

Winter laid its cold hand upon all, and eventually life outside the cave became still. The fresh supplies were mostly consumed by the time the winter solstice had passed. The days and weeks moved on and the people shifted themselves into action once again as the days gradually lengthened. Fishing, wood gathering and stewing food kept them busy.

Spring seemed to dawdle, but the sun made a reappearance so the witan was recalled by Rolf to consider the next stage in the restoration of the village.

Some wanted to return to the old village site, but after much talk over many days Rolf and other menfolk decided they must find a more defensible site and build again there. There were many calls too for the cave system to become the new home base, despite the inconvenience of the hillside location.

Finally, a compromise was reached. Below the cliff was a small bay with a headland that could be reached from their winter home. This headland had views along the coast northwards and southwards, and by erecting their huts and halls on the gentle bay side they could oversee all pathways and tracks in the vicinity. In the event of an attack, the cave system would provide an additional place of refuge and final defence. This decision was endorsed by almost everybody and work on the construction of a proper village started. Each family would construct its own hut or hall and generally give aid to other families, if required. The blacksmith family were the most involved, working to produce and maintain all necessary tools and weapons. They provided service in exchange for building work on their hall and forge. Work started immediately.

CHAPTER 5

Whilst all these decisions and plans were being negotiated and settled, Dana had been making progress in her recovery. A decision was made to permit her to return to the new village in due course.

At twenty-seven years of age she had already been nominated as a possible candidate for the matriarchy. Her time of weakness, undergoing treatment, had not been wasted. Loren had passed on some of her wisdom and knowledge which would be useful if she were to become a village leader and mother figure. One complication might frustrate this proposal, for it had become clear that Dana was pregnant.

Dana herself was not happy. She had been unable to give birth to sons or daughters for Lunn, her husband, but was now carrying a child as a result of rape by a raider. The child would be part alien. Loren had offered the possibility of termination, using potions, but Dana had refused. She had always wanted children, and she decided to carry this through to birth. Dana continued to improve, and by late spring she was able to return to the new village.

Back with her family, Lunn's brothers and friends, she began to bloom and even sparkle as her wit and drive reasserted themselves. The move to village 'mother' was deferred – a fertile woman would make a very welcome contribution to village consolidation. The child might pose a different problem, but they would see how he or she would turn out before any decisions were made about the child's future.

A more immediate problem arose from her position within the village hierarchy. An unmarried woman, with no man or family clan of her own and no obvious allegiances could be a source of friction, competition and discord. Rolf decided Dana would join him at his home fire – after all, his wife and son had been killed in that now distant raid.

Dana was not entirely displeased. She had not considered Rolf a suitable protector, nor was he particularly skilled, but he was pleasant enough. And things had changed: he was now the village leader, after all.

For his part, Rolf was pleased. He had seen how attractive she had grown as her body blossomed, and he had always admired her spirit. The child presented no problems yet, and he looked forward to sleeping at her side. Life was becoming sweet again despite all the changes.

Life in the new village was settling into the traditional patterns, but the raid had given rise to one particular problem. The losses of women and girls meant that there were not enough females in the group. The uncoupled young men were becoming a nuisance, pushing into the families and disputing conjugal rights and sex. Rolf consulted his supporters and a decision was reached. Four young girls, now rather too young, were bought forward. Four troublemakers and five other lads now also entering puberty were called to attend for a selection process.

Each girl was to bed with two young men and share her favours equally and her body willingly. This caused a lot of excitement throughout the whole village, not least amongst the girls who acted as arbiters in the selection. One girl, Renata, decided she would cope with the last lad as an extra, so all was now settled.

For a long time this compromise seemed to be working, and everyone accepted this change. However, Rolf and the elders realised that this situation could not continue indefinitely. Disputes were bound to arise eventually.

Some thought would have to be given to an approach to another village and clan for an exchange of people once summer arrived. The young girls were soon pregnant, and, as carriers of the clan's future, were entitled to extra rations. The hunting teams foraged far and wide, increasing the supply of meat, while the older women foraged for roots, seeds and nuts, and there was milk from goats, sheep and cattle to boost their diet. Fishing in the bay added variety.

The Woman of the Woods and Dana were a great help in these activities. The clan was prospering again.

CHAPTER 6

Dana grew bigger as the baby developed, and soon enough it was time for delivery. Rolf asked Loren to act as midwife, and she was glad to be of help; so she moved into Rolf's quarters straight away rather than disappear into the woods, as was her wont. All the new young mothers gathered daily to talk, either by the well or at Rolf's home. Women do so love to congregate and talk at such times.

Dana and Loren tried to help those who had problems with their children or menfolk, and suggested ways to cope.

"Men are so easy to satisfy," said Dana. "They're just little boys really."

The baby was born to Dana early at dawn on a very bright shining day. It was a boy and he was given the name Aren, taken from Arena, the name for the battleground in an old amphitheatre. He was dark, unlike Dana, and very sturdy.

Rolf was pleased. He had settled into his role as leader and guide to his people; and now that Dana had given birth, he could turn his attention to clan affairs.

The clan desperately needed to grow. The seven families, though now sizeable ones, would not be enough to deter an attacking force. Reivers from Scotland would take anything moveable – even people to sell as slaves – but they did not wish to devastate, just exact tribute.

Forces arriving from Norway or Saxony, in Germany, tended to kill, plunder and destroy, but many youths were abducted to supply slave ships trading across Europe and even into the Middle East. The result was that whole communities were wiped out. They must be resisted.

The moot council met to discuss how they could generate support and, under the leadership of Dana and Rolf, decided they must seek and accept unification with more powerful communities, even if this meant a loss of independence. Rolf was asked to lead a delegation south to seek an accommodation treaty for mutual support. The youths and young men would immediately enter into a programme of rigorous daily training, including cross-country running, climbing and weapons usage (particularly the sword, axe and quarterstaff). Those showing particular aptitude for archery would practise until proficient. This would make the clan more desirable as an ally. Older men and the women would gather wood for a defensive palisade, and rocks for hurling down on enemy forces and to make a barrier on the seaward side of the village.

Plans made, Rolf began preparations for his departure, when he would be accompanied by two chosen men to aid him in his mission.

Dana retired to their hut to care for Aren. As a new mother, she loved to hold him to her breast clad in a swaddling blanket. On the day before the one set aside for Rolf's departure, he entered the nursery area and was surprised at how protective he felt towards Dana and her stranger son. Dana looked up at him, smiled and held out her hand, then, drawing him into her embrace alongside Aren, they cuddled together.

Any distaste overcome, Rolf snuggled down, right alongside her right breast, which was leaking a little from the nipple. On impulse, he took the nipple into his mouth and sucked it clean. Dana gave a little sigh, and a shudder, then held him to her tightly.

Rolf suddenly came to himself and, disgusted, drew away. What was he doing – a grown man taking milk like a baby? But he also became aware that he had a tumescence in his loins. Afire with sudden desire, he pushed Dana away.

She smiled, kissed his hand and said, "Later, darling, but perhaps not before too long."

She understood his need, and he who could have taken any woman realised he now had special feelings towards this older lady.

He rose, needing to get away, and pushed out of the nursing area. To cool his ardour, he decided to take a swim in the bay and made his way towards the beach. On his way he passed the rill where the women washed themselves and their clothes. A solitary young woman was at the stream, bent at her washing duties. She was now kneeling at this task and her arse was raised. He was overcome by heat and walked up behind her.

The girl, Ella, heard him coming and smiled at him over her shoulder. This was just too much. He dropped his codpiece, lifted her kirtle and thrust his penis straight into her body from behind. She gasped, but made no demur and he bucked and thrust until his climax was reached. Ella had climaxed too, but did not pull away and it was only as his penis deflated that he was able to pull out.

She looked up at him, smiled and said "Thank you" as she slipped into the stream to wash.

Rolf was annoyed with himself. Ella was the daughter of the village's main hunter and already the partner of two young men, like the other girls. He might live to regret his action, but still he felt much better, so 'On we go!' he thought.

After a good sleep at Dana's side the day of departure was now upon him. He rode off with a light heart, exchanging quips and jibes with his companions.

CHAPTER 7

Dana grew ever more satisfied with life as the boy Aren grew. He was of average size and, to her eyes, became very handsome as his boyish features took on more character. She often looked to see if he bore any resemblance to the men who had savaged the village, but she had decided that the way he was conceived should not impede her love for the boy himself. He was certainly her son anyway. How would this new life shape up?

Living as the wife of Rolf, the chosen leader, gave her additional status within the village; and as the oldest, most experienced woman, her words and ideas were generally well received. Her main rival and opponent in discussions now seemed to be Ella, but she appeared to be pregnant and a little moody, poor lass.

Life within the village was now fairly pleasant. Bad memories and worries were fading as the new mothers came to terms with motherhood, birthing sons and daughters with little difficulty, but, of course, not without some complaint.

Dana marshalled all these ladies and set up a crèche with the support of the elder ladies, who already looked to her as the matriarch elect. This crèche was greeted with enthusiasm. The new mothers could congregate, talk and give themselves some free time. Their menfolk were already becoming eager for love.

Dana herself faced no such demands, for Rolf was still on his mission moving from one village to the next in search of allies. She missed his company at this time and looked forward to his return.

Rolf, accompanied by his two chosen men, progressed peacefully south. Three men under a flag of truce were not seen as a threat, but none of the nearer villages were interested in an alliance. They themselves tended to look towards Alnwick, Otterburn and Morpeth for support. The lords of these communities were Wogen of Alnwick and brothers Eric and Feodor Brighteyes. It was suggested that he, Rolf, should move on south and west to visit them.

The season for raiding was now in full swing, and Rolf decided to return to his own camp near Craster before proceeding further south. He was disappointed with his lack of success, but he might be needed to lead his men against raiders soon.

Travelling the old road to the north, they came upon several bands of marauders, but stayed off the road, usually camping within the forest edge at night to avoid trouble. They quietly made their way home.

Arriving late in the evening, he went straight to bed with Dana after a quick beer. Aren stayed asleep, thank the gods!

Next day he convened a meeting for the next evening and made a full report. There were murmurs of discontent as he recounted his lack of success. Rumours about reivers' activity were received with dismay, although judging by traditional patterns of behaviour they would be left alone to recover and hoard scarce resources for at least another year.

The forecast early summer came and went by quickly enough, and with a decent harvest they battened down for the onset of winter. Dana was pregnant again. This time, without question, the child would be Rolf's. Aren was growing strongly too.

In the last days of September, a rider brought news of attacks on Morpeth and Otterburn. Feodor had called upon Eric's larger force at Morpeth and they had pulled off a major success. The informant talked of carefully laid plans established by the brothers. Under their leadership a large group of marauders was caught between their forces, which encircled and crushed them decisively. Few raiders were believed to have survived.

For Rolf this news confirmed his decision to approach these lords in the spring.

CHAPTER 8

Winter drew on without incident or a serious mishap, and when the time of dependency on stores, rather than foraging, came upon the families, they all moved back to the cave complex to enjoy warmth and company. The children in particular enjoyed close contact.

Spring was a little early that year, and in March Rolf, Linn and Oli (his chosen companions) returned to their ambassadorial quest, visiting Otterburn first.

Feodor and his clan were at first not very welcoming, for their food supplies were depleted, but when Rolf revealed that he had brought with him a wagon filled with smoked fish, salted meat and storage bins of oats and wheat the mood changed dramatically. A feast of welcome was proposed, and there was much rejoicing in the ranks of Feodor's people.

They quickly settled to negotiations, but Feodor, being the younger brother, could not commit to a treaty without the approval of Eric and Wogen of Alnwick at Morpeth. Feodor would, he said, give enthusiastic support, for he was now convinced the Craster group was wealthy and well provisioned! Feodor, his guards and one wife joined Rolf on his journey south. A messenger was dispatched to advise Eric of their impending arrival and peaceful intentions.

Travelling light without the provision wagons, they made good time and were given a warm welcome by the commoners. Wogen and Eric, the thane, were more reserved and very conscious of their superior status as major lords of the North. Both were considered serious warriors with proven skills in the art of war. More, Eric was clever, a great planner and strategist, whilst Wogen was High Lord of the North.

The clan base camp was huge, well organised and defended, sitting as it did on the top of an old hill fort. It was military in style and in layout. There was still a major road right through the site that connected the two well-constructed gateways. These gates were overlooked by guard towers, and each was constructed to withstand a direct assault. The youths, both male and female, were trained in warlike skills, the men bearing the brunt of any battle and the women effective in support as archers, slingshot exponents and shield repairers. Some were as good as men in the arts of smelting and blacksmith work. Together they made up a formidable force.

Eric had observed the arrival of the party with Feodor and Rolf with some interest. He had already been informed about the purpose of the visit, by the messenger, but he still delayed the first meeting. He had been thinking and planning since the last successful battle and was now considering the establishment of a series of warning beacons along the coastline and the old road north. The beacons would be permanently manned by a watch-sentinel group to provide early intelligence about sea raiders or Scots reivers.

Rolf and his families might make a useful contribution to such an enterprise, but Eric would not disclose his plans until negotiations were complete. What exactly did Rolf want? He called Feodor in to question him.

Two days later, Eric called a council of war and awaited Rolf's presentation. Nervously, Rolf offered to join Eric's band as a vassal in order to procure two things: additional military support in times of trouble and an exchange of personnel. His families were becoming too interbred and needed fresh bloodlines. To this end he would host a midsummer gathering, at which families could meet each other and exchange young folk.

Eric decided this was a sound idea which he could support. His own and Feodor's influence would dominate the east coast north of Alnwick. Lord Wogen of Alnwick also approved, so they all retired to the hall to dine, drink and celebrate.

As a gesture of goodwill, Rolf, Linn and Oli could choose three young men and three young women to accompany them home. This would also be the first step towards integrating their families. All the men were warriors too. They were a bit dubious, but accepted the offer with grace. Eric clearly was already moving on.

CHAPTER 9

Rolf and his guests arrived back at his village to be greeted by every family head. There was an immediate call for a moot, and Rolf was asked to explain in detail the terms offered by Eric and how everyone would be affected.

In general, the families liked what they heard, but some felt the village was being demeaned by accepting vassal status. Others could sympathise with this view, but also understood the need for additional support.

The most heated arguments concerned the young people Rolf had brought back with him. Many believed these folks were putting on airs of superiority and would be troublesome. How did Rolf propose they should be integrated? He asked for time to consult and consider before making detailed proposals.

Several days later, he was still pondering his course of action when the first clash happened. One of the young men of the village had taken a shine to the youngest of the Morpeth girls and she had taken a shine to him, but his bed wife, the lass who had borne him a child, objected, refused him further congress and sent him from her home fire.

This might have passed without incident, except that when the boy, Haden, had joined his new lady, one of her clansmen, Sega, had objected. He struck Haden hard and killed him. Now the killer was held captive. The two women were distraught and, mourning the death, both called for vengeance.

'How very unfortunate!' thought Rolf. 'Now everyone will be taking sides with one group or the other. Pure discord was being sown. He was also called upon to act!

Rolf turned in his distress to Dana. She gave the situation her consideration, called a meeting of all the adult females in the clan and asked the parties involved to explain what had happened in detail. The killer, Sega, was brought in tied to a crosspiece to hear all that was said.

The Morpeth lass, Juno, was inconsolable. She had loved Haden and wanted him by her. She claimed she had never associated with Sega, although he had plagued her before. Haden's wife set her thoughts out clearly. She had two other men to service and felt justified in turning Haden out! The women agreed entirely, and she was dismissed.

The adult females of Craster decided Sega must either die or be banished forever. The girl could stay if she wished, and was asked to be accommodating. If not, she would have to return to Morpeth. Rolf would decide.

Rolf was unhappy that this first experiment in integration should end so badly, but he did listen. He decided Sega must face death by stoning and Juno must be taken home. His decision was final, for he would not show weakness for the future good of all his people, although privately he had sympathy for all involved. His sentences were carried out immediately. Further delay would be intolerable.

He also decreed that the remaining Morpeth men and women should marry each other and settle down to produce children who would integrate more easily than their parents, and, at a future time, add new blood.

Once they were back in their home, Dana asked Rolf why he had decided Sega must die. He explained that it would be difficult enough to get help from Eric's people without having a sworn enemy loose amongst them. He refused to explore his reasons any further, but Dana detected a hint of mistrust in the new alliance.

CHAPTER 10

The reaction of Eric's Morpeth people to the return of Juno and the death of Sega was angry, and Eric decided further acts of unification were necessary to heal the breach.

His two elder daughters were called Una and Chloe. Rolf would meet them and choose one. Then he must marry her before all the clans. Feodor also would claim a bride from Morpeth at the same celebration. Each man would provide a male child of his own family to be held and trained by Eric's warrior teams and to be a hostage to fortune. Once again Wogen agreed.

Eric called Rolf and Feodor to his conclave – no discussion and no resistance would be permitted. They were told they must come straight away, leaving whatever they were doing. Dana and Rolf gave this command some thought, but clearly there was no room for compromise given that Rolf sought aid and alliance. The fraught difficulty would be the hostage boy. They could offer only Aren, for the other child, Benji, had yet to be born. Dana cried, but the lack of an option was self-evident, and so with little or no choice it was decided.

One thing Dana had learned from her days at the crèche was that Ella's son, Daran, was Rolf's, but she could not commit him to life as a hostage without Rolf's consent. She remained silent and prayed to the gods that Aren would be well treated.

The time was moving on, and since Aren's fate was so clearly beyond Rolf's control, Rolf and Aren set off south straight away. Dana cried herself to sleep that night.

Rolf, Aren and Feodor arrived next day tired and cheerless. No welcome was extended to them, although Feodor was lodged well, together with his sister's second son, Jan – his own hostage to fortune.

The very next day the two boys, Aren and Jan, were transferred into the care of the warrior women and bidden to listen and learn.

Rolf and Feodor attended a clan meeting and were introduced to the girls chosen as treaty brides. Eric's oldest girl, Una, made it clear that she felt demeaned. She was a pretty blonde and her figure was full and statuesque. She was an obvious choice, but Rolf felt humiliated by her air of superiority; he therefore chose the second daughter, Chloe, a quiet, rather demure twelve-year-old. Rolf was quite prepared to wait a year before the marriage could be consummated. Chloe would accompany him back to Craster the next day.

Feodor declined Una, a blood relation of his, and chose Una's best friend (another lovely twenty-year-old), who received his decision with grace. Eric approved. He told his brother that this girl was the daughter of another clan chief – she would give him strong sons and extend their family influence further south. A good choice.

A quiet feast concluded the day, which had gone quite well with no obvious display of the hatred many felt towards Rolf. Perhaps the people would now move on and forgive, if not forget.

Eric had been quite interested in one or two of the other girls on offer, and he decided they should both be added to his own female group. Una would be offered to Lord Wogen of Alnwick. Perhaps he would be pleased to receive a ladylike lass with ideas above her present station. Another alliance for the family, perhaps? High-born status was sure to appeal to her vanity.

The next day the two sub-chiefs were dismissed and told to take their new wives home.

Rolf and Chloe left quickly next morning with a small escort. Chloe packed mostly clothes, but also one or two trinkets and her dolls.

On the journey north, Rolf kept wondering how he could break the news of his latest marriage to Dana. She was not his oath wife, but they did love each other and the arrival of Chloe would certainly complicate matters. He need not have worried – Dana was pragmatic. She was at least five years older than Rolf and had been happily married to another man for years. She did now love Rolf and the comfort he had brought her. Rolf was a worthy man, leader of his people. Although the girl, Chloe, would become Rolf's number-one wife in due course, she was very pleasant, quite amenable and eager to learn about life as a villager. Chloe, the daughter of a high thane, had been leading a very contained, disciplined life so far; a bit of freedom would now be her right. She would also be useful when Dana bought her child into the world.

Life at Craster began to resume its normal rhythms. Dana's new child, Benji, was born and grew happily as the years passed.

CHAPTER 11

Throughout these early years Aren and Jan were growing too. The warrior women had their own quarters and, of course, a crèche to take care of their own sons and daughters.

As the children grew, responsibility for training and education was passed from nursing staff to the older children approaching adulthood. These older children were not keen on being given such a task and brought harsh rules into the lives of the 'little ones'. In fact, many of their ideas, commands and rules were contradictory. Jan, a whole year older than Aren, made a point of being difficult and argumentative, pointing out their special status as royal hostages. This earned him many a clout and gradually the hostility of the majority. Naturally, Aren was rewarded with similar treatment.

One big lad, Loden, and his sister, Loren, were particularly vindictive. They together ruled the warrior kids and would personally discipline Jan, beating him viciously on several occasions.

Jan decided to abscond and to take Aren with him. One night, after lights out, they crept from the dormitory, taking their things, including personal items, with them. They raided the kitchens too, taking bread, cheese and some apples, and raced into the woods behind the encampment. They did not think they would be pursued.

In this they were completely wrong. When their absence was discovered next morning, Loden and Loren reported the escape to the warrior leader. She was furious. These two boys were under her control, and if they could not be found immediately she would have to tell Eric. The loss of such hostages to fortune would be severely punished. Jan was, after all, the thane's nephew – the child of Feodor's sister.

All the warrior women, including several skilled trackers, were dispatched immediately to find and bring back the boys right away. Loden and Loren were tied to wheels and whipped for causing this problem. The others in the crèche made it clear Loden and Loren had caused this act of rebellion, and it was not the fault of anyone else.

The hunters and trackers soon spotted the boys' trails through the woods and experienced no difficulty in overcoming any resistance, tying them up like game and returning them to the leader, Leann. Relieved, Leann dealt with them pretty gently, but made it clear any further attempts at escape would be punished severely. She decided that both boys should be given specific duties and placed under the tutelage of the menfolk in the warrior school. Jan (now ten) and Aren (nine) were perhaps a little young to begin training, but better that than to return to the crèche, where trouble would be sure to follow.

The leader of the war band decided to follow Leann's suggestions. Aren was too young yet to begin training in arms, but Jan would join the newest recruits as a junior. He was moved to the war-band dormitory immediately.

Aren was passed into the care of an old former warrior, Bran, who looked after the stable block, the tribe's horses and Eric's two destriers. Aren would work as a stable lad with the other boys until he was old enough to move on up to the training band.

Aren and Jan, who had become companions, were thus separated. Aren was sorry and a bit worried about being separated, but he had no choice except to agree. The other boys in the stable block were unfriendly and kept their distance.

"This kid is special? What rot!"

Aren would get all the dirtiest jobs until he learned his place in the scheme of things.

These two boys, already older than his friend Jan, were often bored. They hated the idea that Aren was different and they did cause problems whenever they were idle – mostly at the end of the working day. When they all were supposed to wash, take an evening meal and then retire to bed, they submerged him in the washtub, took away his clothes to cause him embarrassment, and tipped his meal into his lap whenever the cook and maids were not looking.

One rather hot day Aren had had enough. He faced his tormentors, picked up his stable rake and clouted both lads over their heads. In a rage he tumbled one then the other into the slurry pit, which was quite noxious. As he shouted in glee, he kept prodding them and felled them again into the disgusting sludge.

The lord's ostler, Bran, heard the shouts and threats as he repaired to the kitchen for his evening meal. He strode towards Aren, picked him up, rake and all, and threw him in with the boys. He then hauled each one out, threw them into the horse trough and scrubbed them with a long-handled horse brush.

When all were reasonably clean, he stripped them and told them to go to bed immediately without dinner, but only after first boxing their ears.

That night the stable boys' dormitory was quiet for the first time. Bran slept by the door and the boys knew they could expect trouble on the morrow.

Over breakfast, Bran questioned the farm staff and then interrogated each of the boys. He learned a bit from the older lads and guessed the rest, for Aren would say nothing. The duty of all these kids was to look after the animals and they were told to "Get to it – I'll deal with you all later." He then called in his deputy.

After much discussion, he came to the conclusion that Aren was a troublemaker, but the two older lads should be immediately transferred to other duties within the camp and he would seek out two or three new lads to replace them. Aren would in the future sleep alone in the straw loft and be on call at a moment's notice, night and day.

Aren heard these instructions with relief. He was better off alone with the horses and cattle, he thought. The stable lads could keep to their dormitory and stay out of his way. Word of his testiness and aggression had been passed through the servants' quarters. Given his special status as hostage, he would be given a wide berth in the future.

CHAPTER 12

Life became much more to Aren's liking. He loved the horses and found the cattle no problem, despite the constant milking. He began to make himself comfortable sleeping on straw. He even started to read a book about animal care that Bran had never looked at. He had his meals at a table of his own, and the maids grew attentive as he filled out towards manhood.

The stable for the horses became his special place. Each day he mucked out the stables, then groomed each horse, taking real care over the destriers belonging to Eric and his eldest son, Roman. Bran noticed the change; so did others.

The days, weeks and months passed slowly and the war band had little to do. News of the new alliance had sped throughout the borderlands and few clans of reivers had enough men to challenge such a well-organised force.

The sea raiders were a different matter. Their usual tactic was murder, pillage, rape and the taking of slaves, but their raids were over quickly. They then returned to their ships and sailed away. This affected the smaller coastal villages; and by the time the band reached the scene of devastation, the raiders were gone.

Eric pondered this problem, but could not see a solution. His system of beacons gave notice, but it still took too long to get the war band on site. Perhaps some of the village clans could combine and thereby gain the extra protection they needed. Arranging this would be a demanding task. He decided to delegate the role of leader and coordinator to Feodor, as he was at least family.

Roman, Eric's eldest son, entered and made a counter-suggestion. He volunteered to take over that role. It would be good practice for when the time came for Eric to step aside.

"Yes," Eric agreed, "but first you must talk with Feodor and Rolf, so let us call a gathering for the day of the solstice."

Midsummer came and all the clans gathered together to celebrate. Eric always set a good table and, even as the allies gathered, the cooking fires were in full swing. Pork and lamb were roasted alongside venison and sides of beef. Butchers were busy making sausages, or pie meat, ready for the cooks to prepare. Stewpots bubbled and smelled fine to the hungry guests. Kegs of beer and mead stood ready to be breached, with several tuns already open for serving. An atmosphere of well-being pervaded all.

The Morpeth people were very conscious of their duties as hosts, but the warriors of the war band were instructed to disarm the visitors and act as wardens and peacemakers to the guests.

As dusk approached, Eric ordered out his singers and many musical youngsters joined in song cycles. Then, as a special treat, Eric called in the Welsh band to recount grand stories about gods, knights and ancient wars. Everyone agreed that this was the finest solstice celebration for many years.

The young ones (and some older too) danced in the evening firelight, though many just slipped away to pursue a courtship.

The next day was very quiet for many had overindulged. Some of the young ones took full advantage of the opportunity to slip away again.

Eric called a Moot for later that evening. Many nursed sore heads, but Lord Eric insisted on being obeyed and any straggler was soon rounded up. The reason for the council of war was soon enough explained, then Eric and then Roman set out their defence plan.

Feodor and Rolf decided to go along with this plan. Once again their status was reduced, but the idea of combining people and resources was essentially appealing. The clans had misgivings, but they knew concentrating resources would strengthen them all against marauders. Competition for position and status could be set aside, at least for now.

The families dispersed to talk amongst themselves.

CHAPTER 13

Aren listened to all the gossip carefully and found himself wondering how these changes might affect him. He had met with Rolf and his new wife, Chloe, but Dana, his mother, had remained in the village of Craster to act as 'guardian mother'.

When all the excitement and clearing-away had finished, he returned to his stable duties. It was less than two days since a big destrier, Loki, had taken very ill. Within a day his massive body could not sustain him. Bran and Aren were very concerned, and Eric raged at everybody when he realised that Loki might die.

Bran suggested that they send for the wise woman who lived on the far side of the forest. It was also suggested that Aren should be given the task of contacting her, whilst Bran would attend to the big horse using every skill he had gathered over the years.

Eric agreed. "Get off now, lad, immediately."

Aren chose a good sturdy horse with a bit of speed and departed. He was not too sure where he might find the healer; but Bran had given precise directions and as dusk arrived, so did he.

The small hut seemed rather flimsy, but when he opened the door he saw it was bigger than it first appeared. There was a fire in the hearth, but it was quite low and there was no reply to his calls. He became a little anxious as dusk turned to night. Eric would be pacing the floor and no doubt cursing him roundly.

There was nothing he could do. There was no point in racing about the countryside with no idea where she had gone.

Aren had not thought about food in his haste, but there was a pot of meat and what looked like vegetables by the fire. He smelled the contents and tasted a fingerful. It seemed OK, so he swung the trivet directly over the heat. The lady would surely not begrudge him a small portion.

He sat down on an easy chair by the fire to await the meal. He must have drifted off to sleep, for when he did return to his senses he realised he had company. A rather handsome older woman was standing over him looking annoyed.

He came to his feet swiftly and started to stammer as he explained the reason for his intrusion. The woman proved that she really was wise by letting him babble on. When he finished explaining, she put her hands on his face and explored it with her fingers.

"Ah, a callow youth, then, sent to do his master's bidding."

Aren did not flinch.

"Not so young. And Eric, Lord of Morpeth, needs you to heal his war horse."

"Well, we cannot travel tonight – I will journey with you tomorrow. In the meantime please explain what you know about the horse's condition."

Aren started to talk, but the lady said, "Let us eat first." She then turned and spoke to a young girl standing at the door: "Bring bread and some dishes, then serve the stew."

Aren was shocked. How could he not have noticed the presence of a second woman? He seated himself at a small table; the girl moved slowly and silently to serve him.

The wise woman spoke again: "You may call me Sophie. This girl is my daughter, Sally. Now eat."

The stew was very tasty – better than his meals at camp, and it had a very different flavour. Sophie could not see his expression, but Sally whispered to her.

She then asked, "What is wrong?"

"Nothing," said Aren. "It's just that the taste is unusual."

"That is my woodland herbs and mushrooms. They will not harm you."

The meal over, they settled to talk. The wise woman paid close attention and asked many questions. Fortunately Aren was able to answer reasonably sensibly. Sally talked quietly with her mother, then began to select a number of potions, following her mother's instructions.

Finally, when all was done, Aren was bidden to bed on a straw paillasse, and the ladies settled into their cupboard bed alongside the fire.

They woke early next morning and, after a drink of herb tea, were away by daybreak.

CHAPTER 14

Eric, Bran and Roman were all in the stables when the ladies and Aren arrived. Loki was now on his side and breathing in a panting shallow way.

Sophie took charge immediately: "Out, all of you! No," she said to Eric, "you too. This will take time. Sally, boil some water and bring it here as soon as possible."

Aren led her to the ever burning grate and a big iron pot.

Later that day Aren was permitted to re-enter the stables and go to bed. The two ladies were still working quietly at their ministrations, so he asked what was wrong with Loki. Sophie showed him where the unshod hoof had been split. The soft tissue had been damaged and the fetlock area above the wound had turned septic. There was every chance the horse would soon be affected by the onset of gangrene. If this happened, Loki would probably have to be terminated.

Bran was already getting his stun axe ready to deliver the final blow. Lord Eric would not be pleased, but at least the other destrier, Midnight, would still be available. They would not let Loki die in a painful way.

Aren retired, but slept badly. He loved these big horses. Every time he woke he could hear the ladies talking softly. They were still by the horse's side next morning. All the other horses and cattle had been herded into a new enclosure across the camp. Bran had been careful to see that nothing was allowed to cause them distress. It was bad enough to lose one animal without permitting the spread of fear.

Day after day passed with little change. The ladies had managed to keep the fever down, but the condition could not be cured. At Sophie's request, Loki was dispatched.

Eric was furious, so he looked closely at Bran and Aren. He recalled that this boy was the hostage for Rolf's clan – he had forgotten him over the years. Aren should have been inducted into the war band at least two years ago. Aren was told to report for military training right away.

In some ways Aren was not sorry, for the thought of Loki in his last days had hurt him badly. Action might restore him and assuage his anger.

The ladies were sent home, with a decent reward for time spent, and Aren moved to the new recruits' dormitory under military rule.

CHAPTER 15

Back at Craster, life settled into a pleasant pattern, and for Rolf it was better than at any time in his earlier years. Dana and Chloe were mutually satisfied. Dana's son Benji was growing well and favoured his father in looks, but with something of Dana in his attitude to life.

Chloe was now pregnant with a second child, perhaps to be a boy. The first child, Zoe, was a lovely girl, if a bit precious about her status as 'baby'.

Rolf still spent all his free time thinking about the defence and safety of the clan, which was nearly back to the full complement of twelve families. While the ladies worked the crops, the young men practised for war, foraged far and wide and fished in the sea. When they were at leisure they all liked to be together to socialise, to drink, to dance and to chase the girls, especially on the beach.

The headland site had proved very satisfactory, but the winter home still served as a place of refuge, storage and occasional rendezvous.

Ella had offloaded two of her boys, and would often pass by to be noticed by Rolf. She found him attractive, and of course Rolf was quite aware of this. He already had two wives and was quite satisfied, so he did not pursue her.

His chief concern was about the length of time that had passed since the last raid by the Norsemen. He had heard rumours at Eric's court that the Vikings were raiding further south and that York was their prime target, but a change in the wind could bring them roaring into their tiny bay.

Using his fishermen and their knowledge as an aid, he now

explored the waters of the bay. Rock surfaces, only slightly awash at low tide, restricted much of the access, but there were three clear paths to shore. The two side channels were narrow but navigable, and the centre channel to shore was wide enough to allow safe passage for at least two dragon boats side by side.

Rolf called the fishermen and their wives to a conference to discuss possible defence strategies. One old sea dog recited a story about a time long ago when a raiding fleet had been stopped and trapped by a chain drawn across shipping lanes and then bombarded from heights. He said this action had brought ignominious defeat to the attackers. The youngsters applauded.

For some days Rolf pondered over the story and then called old Rog to see how such a plan could be brought to reality. The villagers did not have chains or even iron to forge one. Rog suggested a wooden barrier.

After several days, during which he mulled over ideas and drew some sketches in the sand, Rolf called his woodsmen to discuss the making of Roman-style crosspiece defences. Three heavy logs, burnt and shaped to a point at either end, were formed into a three-legged cross. A line of these, when ready, would be sunk into the centre channel. These constructions would be bolstered with rocks. A stand of conifer trees nearby would provide timbers resinous enough to withstand immersion in seawater for some years.

The work, once started, went smoothly, and about six weeks later the barricade was completed – but not without complaints from the fishermen, who always preferred the central passage. The two outer channels were much more difficult to negotiate.

In reply, Rolf simply said, "That was the whole point of the operation. Get used to it."

Dana and the village elders eventually agreed the idea was sound. Any vessel reaching the barrier would find its bottom torn out, even at high tide. Clever man! Obviously they had been right to elect Rolf village headman.

Whether word of his defence was carried by informants to the Scots or Norsemen they could not be sure, but another year passed in peace.

Chloe gave birth to another girl, Rae.

CHAPTER 16

Aren had grown quite a bit, and the regular pattern of heavy work in the stable yards had developed his strength and stamina. This was probably just as well, for he was still regarded as an outsider by most of those he was billeted with during training. Each billet hut was shared by about ten trainees, and one who was near to fully trained was put in charge. Given strict instructions about discipline, these 'trustees' ruled their huts harshly. Most of the other men felt they suffered under their 'trustee' and were keen to share their grievances.

In overall charge was an older experienced soldier called Brand. He would not hesitate to break a trainee by any means necessary if that trainee was slack, undisciplined or an aggravation. Beatings, the pillory and the withholding of food were commonplace. Warriors should be strong enough to meet any challenge, so the trainees had to be up at 6 a.m. for their ablutions – nude, of course. Then they were clothed and equipped for a three- or five-mile run before breakfast. A brief break was then given whilst duties for the day were allocated. The warrior band was expected to be self-sufficient and live off the land for the rest of the day. In the afternoon they entered a two-hour period of intense weapons training before being allowed to lunch. In the afternoon, fully loaded with weaponry, they underwent another five-mile run cross-country, including a river crossing, followed by time to pause in a sweaty day (back they went to camp for a substantial meal and then a rest for an hour) before completing the day's chores. Most lads were pretty tired by then, and there was little talk once in their beds.

Routines like this, designed to test the mettle of all warriors, had been learned from the Roman legions and passed on through succeeding generations. Quite a few of Eric's band were descended from former legionaries who decided to stay in Britain rather than return home.

An average boy would become competent under this training in about four to six months. The brighter lads who reached this level quickly could then seek excellence and superior skills through staged competitions, which took place once a month.

The clan elders, including Eric and Wogen, were always interested in these contests – but then, so were all the families involved. Deaths would be mourned, but were accepted provided the contest had been well fought and honourable.

With a regime like this, the trainers were keen to build teamwork and the creation of loyalty to one's colleagues. Steps were also taken to promote rivalry between the three accommodation blocks, which were called Red, Green and Blue. There were thirty-plus trainees in each block. Red was by repute the most successful in competition, although Blue was also handy. Green was the oddball group, but it too had success on a few occasions.

Naturally, Aren had been placed in Green. As he got to know, and perhaps understand, his room-mates he became glad to be in their company. Most Greens were inclined to be relaxed and to talk a lot, and there was even a comic and a novice preacher. The comic, Conn, could be annoying, but kept up morale; the serious guy, Olaf, became a real friend to stand with Aren in times of trouble.

By the end of week four, the first inter-block games were planned. The prize was to be a night off the camp, with food, drink and girls to dance with and perhaps to fool with too. All the teams keyed themselves up and practised the arts of war in preparation. Each team would face both the others one by one, with the winners being the team of the last man standing. Even Aren gave in to boyish enthusiasm and resolved to try his best.

The first games centred on skills – sword, axe, stave and bow. A really skilled lad could enter two games only, so everyone on each team had to show his worth. Death was not intended at these tournaments – the losers must surrender. The judges would signal the end of a contest, and would name the winner if neither contestant would concede defeat. A closely matched pair brought great excitement to the audience.

The team leader for Green was a lad called Brundell, the son of Eric's sister Fran. He was a bit of a lordling and decided he would lead the sword and axe teams.

Olaf was good with a stave, and he took Aren as support alongside Conn.

The last team – archery – consisted of Will, Ben and Hal.

It soon became apparent that the Greens were overmatched. They lost both sword and axe contests to both teams of their rivals. Olaf's group fared better. Aren and Conn lost, but Olaf wielded his stave with real flair and took the winner's place.

The archery contest began with the Blues winning two to one, but the first archer in the red team outdid them all. The Greens got nowhere against either of the other teams.

The Reds, as usual, were declared champions, and celebrated mightily.

CHAPTER 17

The tournament brought about changes in the trainee camp. The trainers tended to be more friendly towards the billet teams, for they themselves would be judged by the quality of their teams. Some easing of controls might help.

Some of the individual winners found their status improved. Several displaced the nominated 'trustees'. In the Green billet, Olaf, the only truly successful trainee, was asked to replace Brundell as team leader, but he declined, preferring to remain with Aren and Conn.

The three friends, like everyone else, began to talk about strengths and weaknesses, encouraged each other and moved closer towards brotherhood. Conn stopped his more outrageous comedies and they all learned he had a more serious side. He told stories of gods and heroes from his Irish forebears and he could sing a variety of songs too. He was always good company in the time before sleep. Olaf was more concerned with issues of justice, honour and care for his people.

Aren paid close attention to both. He had never known brotherliness, nor listened to talk of principles, but he was willing to learn. He gradually began to see patterns in all the actions taken by the trainers, and to discern the moods and frictions motivating his fellow trainees. He hoped he would learn to navigate these troubled waters in due time. He took a decision: he would try to achieve competence in all forms of war, but he would not pursue excellence in any one discipline for its own sake. Observation, he decided, would be his guide.

The second period of training continued as planned, but new

skills were added to the curriculum. Spear and shield-wall tactics were practised daily.

At the end of months two and three, the tournaments took place under full supervision. The skills of all the trainees were improving and the truly skilled warriors were beginning to shine. Leadership in Red, Blue and Green teams moved to accord with new realities.

The reporting and recording of individual performances were controlled centrally within the warrior-band headquarters. Records were kept under the control of the marshal, an intelligent but crippled man who had once been formidable. He, Perce, was in reality the leader of bands that controlled, monitored and defended the clan lands. Even Eric Brighteyes listened to his advice, so Brand reported as accurately and honestly as he knew how.

Perce was always looking for potential leaders, loyal to the clan and its lord, that men might follow in battle. On completion of their initial training, such men who agreed would be offered a period to study tactics under his personal tuition. This chance was given to two men from each team.

Month four brought major changes. All men were allocated to new billets. Every billet would now contain some men from each of the previous teams. There were many grumbles and complaints, but these were summarily dismissed. The war bands must unify.

CHAPTER 18

The final pass-out tournament was a wonderful spectacle. The crowd and the lords all had their favourites, and each of the best and most successful were tested to their limits. On this occasion there were no deaths. Most men knew their closest competitors, perhaps even admired them, so a defeat could be accepted with good grace. The overall champion proved to be Brundell, the son of Eric's niece, but his main rivals were both grandsons: Liam, the nominated heir apparent, and Connor, tall, strong and with flaming red hair – a sign of a close family tie. In the ending parade, the Lord's family thus took pride of place, much to the apparent satisfaction of the clan. The leadership and the succession were in good order.

The finale was called the Choosing. Perce made his selection of six candidates: Brundell, Liam and Connor, of course, then three more, Olaf, Aren and Feodor's youngest son, Bors. Each was presented to the people and later, in privacy, to Eric, Lord Wogen and Feodor. Everyone at this choosing was surprised when Olaf declined. He explained that it was his intention to pursue the career of the warrior priest, ready for action when required, but not to lead men to slaughter. Silence followed his declaration until Eric signalled his acceptance. Another candidate would not be sought.

Aren said his goodbyes in the comfort of his billet and resigned himself to being the only candidate not related to the ruling family.

All the chosen were given two weeks to return to their family homes before the specialist training would start.

Aren had not been home to Craster for nigh on eleven years, but he did like the idea of seeing his mother once again. He was given a steady horse and had the pleasure of being accompanied on part of his journey by Olaf, who planned to begin his wanderings.

CHAPTER 19

The Craster clan welcomed Aren home quietly. Many did not recognise the tall, dark young man at all, but his horse, his weaponry and his superior clothing marked him as a man of status.

It was much warmer and happier for him when he was reunited with Dana and introduced to his half-brother, Benji, whose eyes were full of wonder at seeing his brother as a man full-grown and a trained warrior to boot.

Rolf was rather more reserved. What would life be like if this stranger returned to his world? Chloe was overjoyed to meet someone – almost anyone – who had come from Morpeth. She was only four or so years older than Aren and he was not known to her. Still, she introduced him to her daughters, Zoe and Rae, who retired shyly to peer at this 'wild' stranger from behind a settle. So much for homecoming! Aren realised that for him too much had changed.

Once the feast of welcome in the village was over, everyone settled back into their working routines. Aren decided to wander the hills, forests and coastal areas on the pretext of learning the terrain. He spent more time camping out than back at Craster.

Towards the end of his stay he once again stumbled across Sophie, the wise woman, and her daughter, Sally, gathering herbs and flowers. They invited him to dine once they had established that he was the same person who, as a lad, had visited them.

Sally had grown strong and supple and had filled out nicely, so when they offered him a bed he stayed. It was no surprise when Sally joined him for the night. Several ladies, even older ones, had bedded with him at Morpeth.

Sally was something of a surprise though – a beautiful nude, very mobile and wondrously passionate. They all said goodbye the next day, for he had to return home and then get back to Morpeth for more training.

Goodbyes said, he rode off with a light heart. He was looking forward to learning all he could about the arts of war. His horse could sense his mood and began to prance, keen to run. This was probably as well, for once or twice he spotted men moving along the heavily forested trails. They did not seem to be well organised nor dangerous, but he kept clear of them anyway.

CHAPTER 20

Aren returned to the warrior encampment in a rather constrained mood. His chosen companions from the first Green group had all enlisted in the main warrior teams, and Olaf and Conn had moved away. He had not really enjoyed his time back at Craster, but he had grave concerns about the next phase of training. The only candidate from outside the clan, Aren faced having to study and compete with members of the Lord's family. How could he possibly mix in such company? Eric and Roman were not inclined to be very supportive – still, there was much he could learn from Perce and he would not give up such a chance because he felt vulnerable and exposed. He felt better immediately. The die was cast, and in any case as a potential leader he had his own quarters, a body servant and a cook to attend him.

The days of tactical training began at last; and if anything, the work rate, both mental and physical, was way above the level expected at the lower level. Food and women were at their disposal during any free time, and were provided by the quartermasters on demand.

Aren decided early on not to be too self-indulgent, so worked out with his body servant a simple routine: small meals, a comfortable bath and bed (with the occasional slave girl for company in the bath and bed). He restricted his drinking to beer, mead and fresh water. In his spare time each evening he would walk, run and ride. A fine young war horse named Raven was allocated as his personal possession, and accompanied by a groom too. He had never felt as free from restriction, nor so pampered.

Perce impressed on all the need for care and vigilance, for as a chosen professional each would be under direct scrutiny, both within the clan and by every enemy spy. Pending eventual graduation, each could be the target of flattery, debauchery and subversion. All their tastes, ideas and peccadilloes were the subject of talk and speculation.

They all swore to be careful!

Perce undertook the field training several times a week. They were given maps of the area to be assessed and told to familiarise themselves before actually being marched or driven to the chosen site. Whatever the weather, and especially when conditions were adverse, they were each left to their own devices, and their condition on return was noted in the records.

About six weeks later, each candidate was assigned ten men. These they had to work, train, assess and maintain during each future exercise. Liam and Connor did this well, but Brundell and Bors were a bit too rough on their teams. They were duly reprimanded, much to their disgust. Aren tried to get to know his team, shared their food and shelter, and commended their efforts, but he did not care for slackers and skivers. He asked for two men to be transferred, but was told, "No, you must learn to control the actions of all your team, so get to it." He decided to use peer pressure to bring the two into line.

The next stage involved attacks on fortified positions, each manned and defended by teams from the main warrior groups. The defenders were given plenty of notice of the impending attack and were generously rewarded if they repulsed the attackers. They were fêted if they managed to capture or 'kill' their opponents. Competition was, of course, fierce, and injuries commonplace, even if fought with dummy weapons.

Once these teams had reported the success of their defensive strategy or the reasons for failure, the team leaders were called before Eric, Brand, Perce and their tutors to report success or failure and their explanations or excuses. Liam and Connor had successes to report, but Brundell, Bors and Aren had not captured their target positions.

Successes were praised, failures were explored, and all were analysed to see where faults or problems might arise and what could have been carried out more swiftly or effectively. The apprentices were then graded. Aren was awarded a lowly grade 3, and Bors was awarded a grade 4.

Privately Aren conducted his own analysis. He tried to learn, and practised on his own over the same terrain. He also visited other target areas, and once copies of the reports were made available to all he compared his own solutions with those of his colleagues.

The other four continued to celebrate the conclusion of training in a disciplined way.

Eric, Brand and Perce went into private quarters to conduct a review, the outcome of which would determine the course of the careers of these new men.

Liam and Connor would join the Morpeth force as cohort leaders immediately, ensuring control remained with the family. Brundell and Bors would lead skirmish teams and be responsible for patrolling to the west and north as far as Otterburn. What to do with Aren? Perce suggested he be given the patrol north and east along the coast, where his mettle would be truly tested.

Reivers from Berwick and Kielder, probably under direction from the Douglas and Maclaren families, would, undoubtedly, engage any force which attempted to impede their raids. Additionally, Norse and German raiders always came there first. Aren would undoubtedly fail to meet such foes and overcome them.

Plans now completed, the young leaders were called to muster. Each was given his commission and an outline of his duties, including an instruction to make a full report once an engagement had taken place.

Brand joked, "But only if you live."

Liam privately sought out his grandfather.

"Why did you give the most dangerous duty to the least able – Aren?"

Eric said, "Well, he has an extra incentive because the Craster village falls in his territory. In addition, I do not trust him at all. The further he is away from here the better I like it. He has proved to be proficient with all weapons, but refused to concentrate his skill and excel in only one. He thinks too much. He pays close attention when tasks are allocated, but asks too many questions! More importantly, despite his low grade 3 his men follow him willingly. His ten call him Aren Decimus, and guard him well."

"I fear he might one day usurp your position as chief of this clan."

"Enough! Let him go and do not ask again. I am still clan lord."

CHAPTER 21

Aren was not really deceived by the choice Eric laid before him, but his hostage status had been set aside and he would be free (or at least freer) to pursue his own agenda, for he had learned much and was keen to continue his education. First he would call his ten comrades to him, explore their ideas, and ask for their help and loyalty.

The ten were keen to test their skills. The dangerous path along the north coast was to be their special responsibility, but they would still be serving under him. New ideas were few, but all agreed they would need extra warriors for the average reiver band was about twenty strong and the Norsemen always came in force.

New recruits joined his team because they too craved action; most were related to the original ten. Brand had objected. He agreed extra men were necessary, but his war bands would also have to meet demands from the other leaders of scout groups. The maximum he would offer was a group of ten additional men for Aren's scout group. It was agreed – so be it. The North and East Group set off immediately in high spirits.

Once clear of Morpeth, they were swiftly entering into territory governed by Lord Wogen of Alnwick, so Aren headed east to Dundridge Bay before making camp. Here, once all were settled, he called a meeting. Leaders would have to be chosen and, in the interests of mobility, four specialist teams of five were formed: hunters; foragers and camp builders; archers and swordsmen; and axemen and spearmen.

Naturally, everyone wanted to avoid being in the foraging and camp-building team, so Aren took this important role upon himself. The safety and comfort of the scout group would rest with this team.

Each team was soon established, for the original ten knew their capabilities and those of the new lads. Finn, Karl, Ossa and Gunnor were selected for Aren's team.

Aren talked about tactics too. Twenty men were not sufficient for the task in hand, so they would make an effort to recruit young men with knowledge of the forest and hill trails. They would also need some women for cooking, foraging and comfort; but he insisted they would only co-opt the willing, and even then only with the permission of village elders. He asked that they make a serious effort to help villagers they came across, thus hopefully ensuring safe places to rest and local support throughout this coastal region. He also made it clear that infringement of these rules would not be tolerated.

The next day it became clear that they were already under observation. A small armed force awaited them on the coast road as they approached Amble. Led by a fearsome renowned knight, one Arne Alveson, these men were from Alnwick and they were quite prepared to contest the move further north.

Aren explained their mission was to defend the coastal territory north, between Craster and Bamburgh, from incursion. Lord Wogen of Alnwick, he said, was aware of his mission, discussed in Morpeth, so he asked Arne to stand aside.

Arne was not best pleased. He let them pass, but not without evident reluctance.

"Do not attempt to return again through Alnwick lands without prior permission."

So perhaps all was not harmonious between Alnwick and Morpeth.

'Quite interesting,' thought Aren, who had assumed any treaty had been fully discussed. What would happen if a major invading force came to visit?

As the patrol group moved north they were greeted quietly and without a lot of celebration by village people whose land they visited. Young bloods from several families were keen to enlist, and the force began to grow. Foraging did cause some quarrels as many village elders felt Aren's men were trespassing.

Young women were often keen and liked the look of these lads, but the elders seldom approved. Aren kept the peace, conducted negotiations and agreed to send back any lasses who stole away to them in the night, thus maintaining goodwill. Trust would have to be earned.

CHAPTER 22

The road north now looked clear. Although bands of roughs and displaced men would appear from time to time, few would wish to engage. The group set off at a goodly pace, but kept the scout group forging ahead to warn if danger looked likely.

Within two days they paid their first call on the clan at Morpeth, picked up a couple of young women, both warriors good with bow and spear, then continued on to Craster. Aren had promised to return, mostly because of his mother, but knew another defensive group could not expect to pass Craster barriers without permission from Rolf.

Rolf had grown used to being in command, and although he knew of the formation of war bands to patrol around alliance territories he was not best pleased to learn that Aren reported back to Eric at Morpeth rather than to him. He travelled swiftly to Otterburn to consult with Feodor.

Dana was pleased to spend a few hours with her firstborn son and made him welcome, covering Rolf's absence with a show of hospitality. She was now in her late forties and had moved to special quarters reserved for the matriarch, which were quite luxurious and comfortable. Aren's war band was allowed to camp alongside the former winter home.

The villagers of Craster were eager to feast and enjoy the company of these young men and women. A few wanted to volunteer too, but they would have to await permission from Rolf. They did make an effort at a true welcome. In the meantime Chloe, her children and Benji listened to tales of derring-do and of life at Morpeth with great interest.

Aren gradually became aware of the undercurrents of feeling. As soon as Rolf returned, he organised his men and sought permission for volunteers to join him, which was given. He then departed to establish a base camp near Bamburgh overlooking that rather bleak beach area, so often the docking place for Norse invaders.

It was time to re-establish order, set training schedules and build comfortable quarters before winter set in again. He was a little disturbed that his band, now called the Wolf Cubs, had not engaged the enemy at all, but he resolved to use this respite to train well and keep his lads out of local villages. They were not, as yet, welcome and probably would not be until their efficient defensive capabilities were proven.

He chose a high-level plateau area just behind a coastal ridge as his base, raised his Wolf banner, and erected the sleeping-quarter tents in two lines. He then set his men and women to dig a deep trench around the area, placing the soil removed on the inside edge to create a rampart in the older hill-fort style. The rampart was topped with outward-pointing stakes as a further deterrent.

Foraging was now a priority.

CHAPTER 23

The arrival of Aren's war band and all this activity had been noted. Its strengths and weaknesses had been observed and reported upon. The lairds of the Douglas, McLaren and Munroe clans convened and decided to reinvest these lands. Almost by tradition, these people supplied food, young people and tribute to the reiver clans. They would not brook interference. It was almost as though they were being deliberately challenged and insulted.

Before winter they would therefore make a first attack. Two groups led by tested warriors, each group consisting of about thirty men, headed south. One went via Berwick; the second used the old drove trails until they were south of Craster, from where they would attack north along the old road until they reached the hills at Bamburgh. The two war bands would then liaise and coordinate their move against the Wolf Cubs. They all laughed at this name.

"We'll certainly teach them a lesson, cubs or not!"

Aren's Wolf Cubs made themselves well known. Local villagers were amazed to see groups of armed men and women running past on their daily exercise routine, but soon enough this sight became commonplace. Quite a spectacle to all except to the very young, who were actually employed in domestic duties.

Aren's closest companions, his team leaders, often led the training programmes while Aren himself explored the surrounding countryside with his deputy, Finn Monason, who was an artist with an accurate eye for terrain and a talent for map making.

Finn quickly produced accurate topographical maps of the lands around for about ten miles in each direction. All the team leaders were expected to spend part of their day walking and studying the trackways, the most obvious of which were the droving trails used by the reivers. Many doubted the value of such study, but gradually accepted the routine, although personally they would have preferred to rely on reports from talented youngsters from the villages.

September drifted quietly by in a blaze of autumn colour, and many of the trees and bushes were full of fruit. This harvest was gathered with great pleasure. What they could not eat quickly they turned into preserves for the winter, into cider and fruit beers. Some of these supplies were turned over to villagers, who in return produced mead, to the delight of all the lads.

Days shortened again and October rolled in cold, wet and misty – ideal for tough guys who wanted to creep close and observe the Wolf Cubs' activities.

Aren and his new deputy, Finn, were very aware that a time of trial lay ahead. They were certain that they would be blooded before winter. Expeditions by scout bands with instructions to watch for intruders took the place of the morning runs.

It was during one of these early morning expeditions that the first skirmishes occurred. The reivers' laird, one Colin Munroe, could not resist the temptation to strike the first blow against the last scout group to depart on that fateful morning. His logic was reasonable: the camp would be at its most vulnerable when the scout groups had left the Bamburgh site.

"Let them go, then attack in force."

In fact, his attack force had already been spotted the previous day and every move he made was being reported back to Aren and Finn. Aren ordered the skirmishers out, but then told them to swing left and right to take up positions behind the reivers' band. Once Munroe's force committed itself to attack, it met a strong defence force and was itself attacked on all sides from the rear.

The attacking force managed to break through the ramparts and cross the ditches, but could move no further. Men were felled on both sides of the defensive ditch. A small number of reivers managed to escape by retreating into the surrounding woodland, and, unfortunately, Colin Munroe was amongst those who got away.

News of the attack and its outcome was soon circulating in the nearby villages, and word was transmitted north to Berwick and the reiver lords.

The infiltrating band which had advanced up the Roman road from the south was recalled quickly, before further losses depleted the marauders' defensive capacity.

The orders given were specific: "Reivers, return home and prepare for a spring offensive next year."

When Colin Munroe and the other survivors arrived back at Berwick, he was arraigned before the full council of lairds to explain his actions. Why had he disobeyed his instructions and attacked alone?

Colin pleaded his case. He said he saw an opportunity and took it! The other lairds were not impressed. He had ruined their plan, lost men and had, in fact, proved that the Wolf Cubs were a credible fighting force. He would never lead again.

Munroe did not appreciate his demotion, and seeds of dissent were sown in the wider groups.

Aren decided his group would not revel in their victory. He knew the Scots would not let such an insult be forgotten. They would be bound to return in force sometime soon, or lose control of their supply sources in the area. His Wolf Cubs must remain on alert even through the approaching winter days.

Locally, things did improve. Many of the village elders around them promised help and some supplies to help feed the cubs through the winter, as long as their support was not talked about. Aren thought this attempt at secrecy was foolish – the reiver spies were everywhere – but kept his thoughts to himself. His men would need all the comfort they could get.

CHAPTER 24

That year winter was particularly severe. First there were heavy frosts, then snow for days on end. Long before the winter solstice all roads and trails were enclosed in banks of snow. Where winds piled the snow into drifts some were as deep as their horses were high. The enemy stayed home.

The Wolf Cubs still exercised. Aren had commandeered a longhouse in the nearest village, as an exercise room and sleeping quarters. The village elders were not happy about this, but did not offer more than token resistance. Pillage had anyway reduced their manpower to low levels – there were few younger menfolk left. The wives and daughters made it clear that fit young men and a few women would much improve their future prospects.

The Wolf Cubs were grateful and much in need of diversions. Village life now coalesced around the longhouse.

It was only natural that disputes and misunderstandings multiplied in such a closed atmosphere. Aren and Finn took turns to sit, talk and eat at the community tables, and each day a court of inquiry sat for two hours to listen to complaints and arbitrate. Infringement of the conditions set by this court would be punished severely by loss of possessions, loss of status and, worst of all, isolation and shunning. Further disobedience would be punished by death. Fortunately, few contested the judges' decisions.

Liaisons were encouraged – the Wolf Cubs and the villagers needed children to guarantee any sort of future – but strict codes of discipline were set and rigidly enforced. Aren could not allow too much dissension to arise from this potential source of conflict. Over the winter two Wolf Cubs and one village girl were executed under this regime.

Once the signs of spring returned, everyone took opportunities to seek privacy – some solitary, and others in newly formed liaisons. All were glad to return to the warmth and comfort of the longhouse at night.

The days lengthened and by the spring equinox the scouts reported increased enemy activity along the raider trails. Hunger alone would ensure that raids would begin at any time now.

Aren called a muster, sought out his team leaders and restarted the fitness training programme in earnest. It would take a week or two to bring the men back to condition and alertness. However, one dynamic certainly changed: most of the Wolf Cubs now had commitments to village girls or women, some of whom were young widows. They wanted to establish more-permanent quarters and improve both security and maintenance in their new home area. Some men, like Aren, were still solitary and without settled commitments, but this was becoming unusual, and each of them had received notice of a need to liaise more willingly and settle down. Uncommitted men, like untaken girls, were more likely to cause trouble.

Aren decided he himself must settle, but with whom? Several young ladies from villages nearby had been paraded, but there was only one lass he fancied to bed regularly. She was a Scottish lass taken in some raid as a child. She, Lana, was willing, but her master still wanted her for himself.

The elder women of the village decided his stand-off was fraught with danger. They called the girl's master to their counsel and told him he must surrender his interests to the wishes of the community. Aren, they said, was too important to slight. He, Ronald, gave permission for Lana to move permanently to Aren's side, but reluctantly. He would find a way to salvage his pride later.

Lana gave great satisfaction as an oath wife, but she missed one of her village friends, Elain, very much. Elain was untaken. She was rather skinny and not well endowed, but had a keen mind and loved to sing as she worked. It was this comforting sound that Lana missed almost as much as the girl herself. Aren gave permission for Elain to join them.

It is almost impossible for people and lifestyles to continue unchanged, and this new community was developing in ways Aren had never considered. Family men setting up and building homes for their dependants did not want to commit so much of their time to training, and a certain degree of slackness in vigilance was becoming obvious.

The marauders soon provided the antidote by raiding into the area. The west winds of March brought a whole fleet of problems. Raiders from Scandinavia came over the horizon and headed for the beaches at Bamburgh.

The coastal warning beacons were lit and a rush of flames sped south, alerting Ross at Craster, Feodor at Otterburn and Eric at Morpeth. The different skirmish groups were called to coalesce and advance on Bamburgh.

Aren's Wolf Cubs could not prevent so many raiders from beaching their dragon ships, but they did make the landings difficult. Catapult-launched rocks and fireballs were hurled at any vessel within their range. Several Viking vessels were lost, and armed men swimming ashore were very vulnerable. Most boarded other dragon ships. The Norsemen were annoyed. Who were these defenders? They would pay with their lives for such impertinence!

Most of the fleet vessels stood off, and plans were set for a mass landing along all beaches in the area after dark. The best warriors would lead them in, secure a beachhead and overcome all resistance.

The first skirmish group to arrive this day was led by Bors' lads, who had set out immediately from Otterburn. Before full dark, thirty men from the Iveston band arrived, led by Blundell. These men were all experienced in fighting the reiver bands and were most welcome.

Aren greeted his war-band brothers with enthusiasm. Their support would make a real difference in the coming hours. He deployed his forces high above the beach area and set spear, javelin and bowmen along the lines at regular intervals, taking care to overlap the fields of fire. A breakthrough by Vikings would be met by a unified shield wall of armed men. Like the Vikings, all warriors would be on foot.

Light faded and the enemy made their move: six ships headed

straight for shore, with three other ships on each side, slightly north and south of the main attack group, led by Haggar Olafson.

Aren, using light from beacons and firepits, deployed his force to meet the first sallies. His men were fearful, but determined to repulse each attack. How successful would they be?

The Vikings hit the shore directly, then were out of their vessels and racing across the sands in seconds. Their war cries and shouts echoed like banshee wails along the coastline.

The first shock of contact was confused and frightening. Some Vikings simply ran straight in, swinging axes, swords and pikes. They hit like a herd of bulls, but the defenders had locked shields in defence. Many were caught by long-shafted weapons, pulled down and killed, but not without losses to the Vikings.

Using agreed signal calls from conches and bullroarers, Aren called in support from the wings and was rewarded by the sight of his men retaliating. Few Vikings from the first wave survived.

The enemy force reeled back. The defence was stronger and more able than they had expected. It was time to regroup, combine units and attack at a steady pace. They would break this lot or die in the attempt, but the leader acknowledged they had never met such determined resistance before.

Moments passed as both forces drew breath and prepared for the next clash. While they stood there, a slight figure appeared on the headland and a voice rang out high and clear – a skirling song of victory and death. Aren recognised the voice of Elain raised to full volume. The men stood, heads down, listening to this song of loss and love. All – Viking and defender – were moved.

As the song faded battle was joined, but now it was different. Slowly, deliberately the enemy advanced in close order, growling their own songs of victory and defiance.

The resulting clash was harsh, punishing and unforgiving, with neither side prepared to consider retreat. Death reaped the field. The toll of Aren's men grew ever larger, but the attacking force stumbled. There were no reinforcements for them. Apart from a small watch, every vessel had been stripped of men to form the fighting force.

Haggar looked around him. His own bodyguards lay dead or dying. Few recognisable warriors were left (most were injured or mazed in some way) – so few that they could never now raise another raiding party. He signalled to his conch man and gave the signal to call the retreat.

Aren, Bors and the remaining defenders watched them leave. They had no heart to pursue these men, all of whom had fought well and their courage deserved recognition. A cornered man without hope would be a dangerous opponent. Aren signalled the bullroarers to signal disengage!

The enemy were allowed to gather their dead as a gesture of respect.

CHAPTER 25

Many of the village elders wanted to celebrate this victory, but so many men had been lost that more homes were in mourning than were inclined to rejoice. Aren's Wolf Cubs had lost thirty-five men and were now only a token force. Blundell and most of his skirmishers were dead. Those still alive had teamed up with Bors' men – the largest group left alive. Their lives spent patrolling the Kielder Forest had forged them into a great team, which worked well as a unit.

After a few days of rest, Bors and Aren prepared a full report for Eric and Liam at Morpeth. Bors had enough men left to man the reiver defences here while Aren delivered their joint report to the council there.

Aren needed new recruits to join his Wolf Cub units and must plead for support from his base camp, and its leaders.

Before he was to leave he gave himself a few days to rest and have one or two injuries attended to. Lana was particularly attentive and used skill to tend him, then surrendered to his passion. Elain stayed away the first night back, giving them time for reunion. Aren looked upon her quite closely when she did come back. She looked and behaved exactly as she had before, but her songs awoke memories of the battle and he closed his eyes to relive one or two specific incidents. Looking back soon led him to raise questions of himself. Could he have been victorious without such a large loss of life?

He awoke next day, resolved to move south. There was so much to do he had no time for introspection and analysis now. Perhaps later. He packed, picked his escorts and left.

The journey south and west passed without incident. News of the Viking clash had become common knowledge.

He thought, 'My gods! Word does travel fast. Now even Eric and Liam must know exactly what has occurred, and that I am travelling to seek support.'

He was not wrong. The leaders at Morpeth were at that moment in council discussing their next move.

A tremendous crowd had gathered at the clan hall and the noise of the welcome extended to Aren reached Eric quickly. He composed himself, called Liam and moved out to make this man feel welcome. He had won this first battle, after all.

Aren was met, clasped warmly and given time for a bath before the evening feast and festivities. All was sweetness and light as cheers and plaudits rang through the reception hall. Hail the conquering hero indeed! A night of excessive eating and drinking did not really please Aren, but the conventions had to be performed as expected.

He was given the next day as a day of rest while all about recovered from their indulgence. So he stripped, swam in the river and set off for a run through the bright, beautiful countryside with his old dog Ruby panting at his side. She was getting very grey in the muzzle since he had been away. On the way back he stopped to swim and sat with Ruby stretched out sopping wet beside him, nuzzling his hand and enjoying a stroke and a cuddle.

The time for the war-council meeting arrived all too soon. As Aren entered with his guards, one each side, the buzz of conversation stopped. Eric called, rather unnecessarily, for order and invited Aren to speak.

Aren had been pondering over the events and sequences by which battle had been joined, and his detailed report was received in complete silence as each elder tried to picture the conflict. At the end of his report Aren handed over a written report from Bors. The seal was still intact. Eric nodded his thanks and called for questions.

Slowly, after a brief silence, those points which Aren had expected were explored. Could he and his men have prevented the landings? Why were the Vikings not met as they stepped through the surf and made their way ashore? Men are particularly vulnerable at such a time. Why did Brundell and his team get into trouble? Was it for lack of support?

Aren considered each point as it was raised and gave his answers. The most difficult to explain was the collapse of the left wing under Brundell. He gave his considered opinions. Brundell and his skirmish group had patrolled the area around Wooler and had not really been tested to the full. There were murmurs and mutterings as he made this point. Brundell was popular.

Next he opined, "The Viking force under Haggar struck the centre, but his most experienced warriors were placed on the right wing, opposite Brundell. They extended their line, overlapped Brundell's team, and swung left, attacking from the front, the side and, later, the rear. His group did well in defence, but was simply overwhelmed."

Silence reigned as each man visualised this situation. Then more questions.

"Could this move not have been foreseen and countered?"

"Yes, if I had had foreknowledge of such a move. I did not think it possible."

Eric dismissed Aren. The council would now consider its verdict. The arguments, shouts and disagreements erupted even before Aren had left the hall.

Several days passed before Aren was called to hear the council's views, but Liam did pay a call and stayed to eat as a sign of his personal support.

Aren found himself quite isolated during these days. Left to his own musings he found time to mourn the loss of friends, including so many of his young Wolf Cubs. He did not care what the war-council decision was; his own conscience was enough of a burden.

When finally called to attend, he was cool and listened to their decision without emotion. They decided he had performed his duty well overall, but they had reservations about his ability to carry out the responsibilities of a field marshal and influence the course of battles. However, no one else had volunteered to take over from him – not even Lord Alnwick's most able man, Arne Alveson, nor Roman, the marshal at Morpeth.

Aren was invited to return north, resume control in the Bamburgh area and try to learn from his mistakes. He could pick a team of twenty men maximum from the Morpeth war band, subject to final approval by Perce. He accepted. He had had his fill of Morpeth.

CHAPTER 26

Returning north, Aren decided to follow the road and trails that would lead him to Wooler. Now that the skirmish team led by Brundell had fallen, he wanted to see for himself what life was like amongst the people living there.

This turned out to be a fortunate decision. The leaders of the Wooler communities were in turmoil. News of the battle and the losses sustained had increased local tensions and uncertainties.

As a consequence, when news of his approach was made known many turned out to greet this new overlord. A woman offered herself and her daughter as comforters, and Aren was pleased to accept their offer of a proper feast. Celebrations would be staged the next day.

Aren spent a comfortable evening enjoying food and a bath in the local stream before retiring. The lady herself joined him.

The feast was well attended and all the local headmen came from villages around to pay their respects. Aren learned all he could about raiders, marauders and conditions regarding food and safety in the area.

The following day, after giving thanks to the people of Wooler generally, he gave his compliments to the lady, and left. The Wooler families decided they liked this new rather undemanding 'Dark Lord'. His black hair curled down his back and his direct intensely black eyes looked intriguing, even if a bit menacing, and set the ladies talking.

Back at the Bamburgh camp all was in order. Bors and his men had cremated the remains of the Wolf Cubs, and village wives had cared for the injured under the supervision of the matriarch. Some girls and the children were still in mourning; they all turned out to welcome Aren home, though many wept.

The arrival of the twenty reinforcements brought a bit more life back to the place, and as the days passed things in the villages around began to return to normality.

Bors and his band left the next day, for they had to get back to Otterburn, where duties awaited them. Most of the original Wolf Cubs stayed with Aren, and he was glad of their instinctive and constant support. They brought discipline to the Morpeth men too, for their actual battle experience entitled them to respect. Adjustments would be required to incorporate the new men.

Finn started up the daily exercises and drill as a way to achieve some coherence quickly. Aren approved and took care to join them each day, as a personal discipline. He quickly got the measure of the new men and soon appointed Luc Thorsen as a skirmish team leader; others would follow in due time.

The most pressing matter was the unguarded post at Wooler, so after some consultation with Finn he appointed his old bodyguards, Ossa and Karl, as leaders of a small team of fifteen, mostly to be made up from men from the Wooler area itself. They had to learn to contribute to their own clan defences.

Both guards were sorry to be leaving Aren, but understood the need; the work needed to be done, and the two men would support each other well. First though they had a quiet word with their replacements, emphasising vigilance and their duty of care to the Lord.

It takes time to bed a new team in, and the Scots were well aware of all that was taking place at Bamburgh. Douglas and Frasier decided to risk a foray south – they dispatched two teams of a dozen men each to act as harriers.

"Strike and retreat, strike and retreat, pulling in the inexperienced, then reverse and strike, attack and kill."

Tactics such as this are difficult to combat and can influence morale adversely. Direct confrontation with the main defence force was forbidden, at least for now. Local Scots sympathisers were to be encouraged and rewarded.

These raider teams did work efficiently. The territory south of Berwick and down the coast towards Bamburgh became unsettled. Crofters, villagers and other small communities all faced real uncertainty. Raids were frequent, but not regular. Boys, girls and women were often injured or killed. The men hardly dared leave home each day for fear of a strike. If they did go out, to farm, forage or hunt, death pursued them. A stream of people arrived daily at Aren's base seeking safety.

Aren guessed this provocation was planned to draw his force into action immediately, before cohesion was achieved. He gave close attention to those men and women who had personally seen the raiders in action, and he learned that two separate small skirmish forces were active. He decided to act immediately.

Leaving Luc behind to continue with the training programme, he took a dozen of his remaining Wolf Cubs, including four archers, and a local forester into the surrounding forest. Success had made the reivers confident, and one group decided to strike inland a bit further, crossing the old road to do so.

This was a mistake. Aren's force had just entered the same area to sweep the land from the west, as the raiders had been spotted here once or twice before.

The reiver commander, Alun Frasier, and his men took few precautions to move quietly and were met head-on. Their first sign of Aren's men was a rain of well-aimed arrows, which killed two men and felled another three. As they closed ranks in nearby woodland, Aren's main group struck. Only one injured raider, a lad, got away to give warning to their brother group. Alun Frasier was cut down by the Dark Lord himself.

Leaving the dead where they lay, Aren swung his team north. His tracker, the woodsman Dann, quickly found the trail left by the injured lad. Aren and his team followed, but kept well back hoping he was heading towards some agreed rendezvous point. He was, but actually died before he reached his destination. Aren sent out his scouts in twos with instructions that if the marauders were spotted, one would follow to keep them under observation while the faster man or woman would return to report.

The scout groups were self-sufficient, but Aren was growing concerned. It was three days before a runner made it back. The woman, Heidi, talked quickly. The trail she and another scout had found led them straight north. It was clearly the trail left by the reivers as they moved south some time before, so the scout, Johan, decided to wait alongside this clear route rather than wander. The reivers' skirmish band had passed Johan's observation point about two hours ago. Heidi had run and walked to deliver this message quickly.

Aren asked if she was fit enough to return to Johan now. Yes, she replied, so his band left with her immediately.

The reivers had had about four or five hours' head start by the time they reached the observation point, but Johan had moved on, presumably following at a discreet distance.

Moving swiftly, but with due caution, they realised the enemy had already passed through the outer defence ring formed by the Berwick bands. They stopped and bedded down for the night, but posted sentinels first.

The days passed, and at last Johan returned. He had trailed the raiders right into Berwick, but very discreetly. He entered a pie house and had a meal there, but no one seemed interested in him. The place was full of strangers, most carrying some weapon or another, and he blended in carefully.

Conversation around the tables and later the fireplace confirmed that the destruction of one reiver band in the south was common knowledge. The Frasiers were in a rage at the killing of the laird's youngest son and a punitive revenge strike against Bamburgh was inevitable. There were mercenary adventurers who would join in any assault, and there was much boasting about conquest and the rewards this would bring. These mercenaries simply loved war and conquest. Perhaps they thought moving south would be easy.

Aren dispatched two runners by separate routes – one to Eric at Morpeth, the other to Bors and Feodor. It was time for the associated peoples to demonstrate their worth.

CHAPTER 27

Aren settled in on a heavily wooded hill just beside the Great North Road and rested his men. He called Finn and together they studied Finn's latest rough map of the surrounding area. They decided this camp was well sited, reasonably safe and not too easy to stumble upon. They could await developments here for at least a few days.

They also talked together about their ideas regarding future reiver action, eventually agreeing that Berwick men would be quite reluctant to field an army and seek confrontation. All their experiences to date seemed to show that reivers preferred to operate in raiding and skirmishing groups, terrorising farmers and collecting tribute. They had little experience of pitched battles. Still, given the anger and bitterness of the Frasiers, anything was possible.

Aren gave the subject more thought overnight. The whole purpose behind the move by Eric and Lord Wogen of Alnwick had been unification and pacification. It was hoped that the training of noblemen would lead to more liberty and safety from attacks. Peace would bring hope, growth and greater prosperity to their people.

Now the whole border area was aflame with anxiety and fear. Further action by marauders would exacerbate the tensions. What could Aren do to avoid an onslaught? Only one possible course of action might bring some reduction in the obvious tension felt on both sides of the border: a personal challenge to combat.

He called Finn, explained his decision and sent forth a herald carrying a white flag and Aren's personal banner – a single black wolf on a blue ground – to convey his challenge to Frasier and Douglas.

He offered personal combat to Frasier, to Douglas or to any champion nominated by them. In the event of his challenge being accepted, war itself would be averted. Peace was hopefully the alternative.

Aren had caused them damage and in his way he offered them what he hoped would be sufficient redress.

The Herald returned without an answer. The reiver lords would meet, consider his offer and report in due course. Berwick was awash with rumours of his challenge.

The lords met in closed session; their advisers had been dismissed. This challenge was a matter of honour and pride. The Scots were hard men and never had they refused to meet a challenge. Failure to do so now would impugn their reputation and might impact upon the loyalty of their men.

Neal Frasier (the laird's eldest son) and Connor Munroe (the Douglas champion) would accept the gauntlet on behalf of the clans. Who was this upstart anyway with his banner of ill omen? Reivers had ruled this coast in all but name for over 100 years.

A herald was called, given a message, and under the flag of truce he delivered it together with the mailed gauntlet thrown down by Aren. The arena would be on Berwick Fields – a training area just outside the city. Spectators would be welcomed and all would be given vows of personal safety. The venue for the field of honour was accepted without demur and the date, one week later, was accepted.

CHAPTER 28

By the day of the contest, Berwick was alight with anticipation. Eric, Roman, Feodor and Bors had all arrived to witness the event and the city ramparts were crowded with spectators. Privately Eric was astonished. He had always viewed Aren with suspicion and this grandstanding proved that he was right. Even if he died, Aren would be remembered.

The tournament weapons had been placed upon a bench covered in red cloth. The choice was impressive: swords, long, short and curved; claymores, of course; daggers from a number of countries; shields, but all of the small buckler style as the audience wanted to see the combatants clearly; axes, single- and double-bladed; and spears, all again short. Many amongst the crowd had admired these and speculated about how they might be used. The contestants could make a personal choice. All the weapons were wickedly sharp.

Aren's first opponent was to be Neal Frasier, who had personal reasons to seek revenge. Aren gave him first choice at the weapons bench. He chose a long sword and a dangerous-looking axe. Aren chose a dagger and a version of the Roman short sword. They then faced each other and awaited permission to engage. The tourney trumpet sounded.

Frasier was light on his feet and moved with speed, first a quick swing, then a pivot and a thrust with his long sword. Aren parried both and fell back. He watched carefully as his opponent began a series of moves which he countered with some difficulty. Like in training at Morpeth, he was letting his opponent dictate the pattern. He was running through his repertoire too. Suddenly

Frasier began to be more successful. He switched tactics to a high guard and chopped downwards at Aren's neck. As he passed with the axe and brought it back on the backhand, Aren leapt in under the downward swing and got his body close to Neal's, then thrust upwards with his dagger, piercing his opponent's axe arm as it moved in its swing. The dagger stroke was lethal, cutting through muscle and causing blood to spurt from the severed artery above the elbow.

Frasier swore, dropping the axe from nerveless fingers, but he then pivoted and his sword cut into Aren's thigh. Fortunately this sweep was not powerful enough to cut through his opponent's leather thigh pads completely. It caused damage, but had not severed his leg.

With both men now blooded, the fight slowed. The blood loss alone was enough to weaken Neal, whilst Aren had lost some mobility. The spectators were yelling for blood. Medical help was granted. Neal's arm was bound to stop further blood loss, and some salve was brought for Aren and a tight bandage was applied.

The judges asked if the contest should proceed and both men agreed. From then on it was a grim affair, both trying to inflict a mortal blow. The loss of blood had clearly slowed Frasier, and eventually Aren managed to chop down through Neal's helm, inflicting major wounds to his head and neck. The neck wound alone bled copiously.

Aren stepped back, lowered his sword and dagger and looked at Neal, now down on one knee with head flopping. Then Frasier raised his sword and dropped it at Aren's feet in surrender. Aren clasped his extended hand, saluted and turned away.

The marshal of the tourney gave a signal and disengagement was sanctioned. Respite overnight was agreed, but Aren would face Connor Munroe tomorrow as planned. In any event, Connor had refused to engage the enemy in a weakened state. His honour would be sullied. The crowd were a bit disappointed, but felt due punishment would be inflicted on their enemy next day, so they retired to talk, debate the contest so far and, of course, drink.

Eric sent his doctor to check on Aren, but his help was refused. Finn had sent for Dana once the challenge had been thrown down. She had come and brought Sally, the present wise woman, with her. Together they removed Aren's padded coat, cut his pants and knee guards off, then bathed him, massaging oils and salves into his open wounds and bruises. Sally then got him to drink a powerful sedative to put him to sleep. Both ladies sat by him all night, monitoring his condition.

Next morning, he was very stiff and could not remain on his feet for long – not the best condition in which to engage in combat. Again they bathed him, oiled him and gave him a combination pick-me-up. Aren began to feel better quite soon. The challenge would be taken up again at midday.

By noon the battleground was crowded with lords, their retinues and hundreds of other spectators. Connor and Aren entered the arena together and the crowd screamed in their excitement. Connor was at least half a head taller than Aren. His arms, chest and thighs look massive under their leather padding. Aren was tall and slim, and looked almost boyish beside his opponent.

They approached the weapons bench together. Connor chose weapons of great power – a broadsword and a massive war hammer. Clearly he intended to batter his opponent to death. Aren decided his only hope lay in athletic speed and accuracy. He chose a short Spanish sword with a double edge and a small German spear with a blade-like head almost twelve inches long, which he would wield like a quarterstaff as Olaf had taught him.

They lay on with a will once the signal blast roared out, Connor whirling wide swings while Aren constantly threatened to pierce and sever.

Such combat seldom lasts long after the initial flurries, and nor did this bout. The final clash showed both men had stuck with their original ideas. As Connor swung the broadsword at Aren's head, he, Aren, slashed with the bladed spear piercing and cutting along the forearm of his opponent and stopping the swing in mid stroke. Connor, however, was already in motion and the war hammer in his strong left hand crashed with incredible force against Aren's right upper arm and shoulder.

Aren sank to his knees in excruciating pain and made one last despairing thrust with the spear in his left hand. It rose swiftly, slipped under the padded doublet, pierced Connor's chest from below, tore through muscle and intestines, and went on until it reached his heart. Connor too fell to his knees, but he was dead long before he hit the ground.

Aren lay unconscious, completely unaware.

There was a stunned silence as the audience realised the contest was over. They waited for the winner to rise and claim victory, but no one moved in the arena. The pool of blood grew ever wider. There was no true victor, then. So quietly they dispersed, talking of what they had witnessed.

Finn and the Frasiers carried the fallen men from the field. A doctor was sent to Aren's tent because he, at least, was still alive. When he saw the damage caused by the hammer blow all he could do was amputate the right arm, then try to re-form the cracked and broken ribcage and bind this together. He did not think the man would survive, but he was young and fit.

Dana and Sally had come again to his bedside, but there was little they could do except bathe and clean his body. He did stir, open his eyes and smile, then pain hit and he fell unconscious again. Dana decided that his comrades should take him back to Bamburgh by wagon, or carry him there themselves. His companions, acting on orders from Finn, arranged to carry him home in a litter. A wagon was far too unsteady and would only cause further damage. The procession left Berwick and moved slowly and steadily along the Roman road.

Aren did not complete the journey, but died somewhere along the route, although the exact point of death is unknown.

The funeral was well attended. His former comrades came in force. They built a massive pyre on the beach, then placed his body on it and his last weapons alongside him.

Once alight, the pyre burned for a whole day. The voice of Aren's second wife, Elain, rose in oblations and dirges for over an hour in order to accompany his spirit as it rose to the heavens.

Over 150 years later, they still told stories of the Dark Lord around campfires along the north shore.

NOTE: Human beings have a tendency to remember heroes and forget to praise those who design and plan for peaceful cooperation.